MOUSE'S FIRST HALLOWEEN

Lauren Thompson

ILLUSTRATED BY

Buket Erdogan

SCHOLASTIC INC.

New York Toronto London Auckland Sydney
Mexico City New Delhi Hong Kong

To
Owen
L.T.

To my
daughter,
Yagmur
B.E.

Published by Scholastic Inc., 555 Broadway, New York, NY 10012,
by arrangement with S & S Books for Young Readers, Simon & Schuster
Children's Publishing Division. SCHOLASTIC and associated logos are
trademarks and/or registered trademarks of Scholastic Inc.

12 11 10 9 8 7 6 5 4 3 2   1 2 3 4 5 6/0

14

Printed in the U.S.A.

First Scholastic printing, September 2001
Book design by Heather Wood

ISBN 0-439-31240-X

One spooky night
when the moon was bright,
Mouse crept around,
and this is what he found....

High in the sky,
Mouse saw
something flying—
Flit! Flit! Flit!

"Eeek!"
Mouse
squeaked.

What could it be?

Swooping bats!

That's all.

Not so scary after all.

Down on the ground,
Mouse heard something moving—
Rustle! Rustle! Rustle!

"Eeek!" Mouse squeaked.

What could it be?

Tumbling leaves!
That's all.
Not so scary after all.

Up on a pole,
Mouse saw
something flapping—
Flip! Flip! Flip!

"Eeek!"
Mouse squeaked.

What could it be?

A waving scarecrow!

That's all.

Not so scary after all.

Under a branch,
Mouse heard
something dropping—
Plop! Plop! Plop!

"*Eeek!*"
Mouse squeaked.

What could it be?

F_all_i_ng _app_l_es!

That's all.

Not so scary after all.

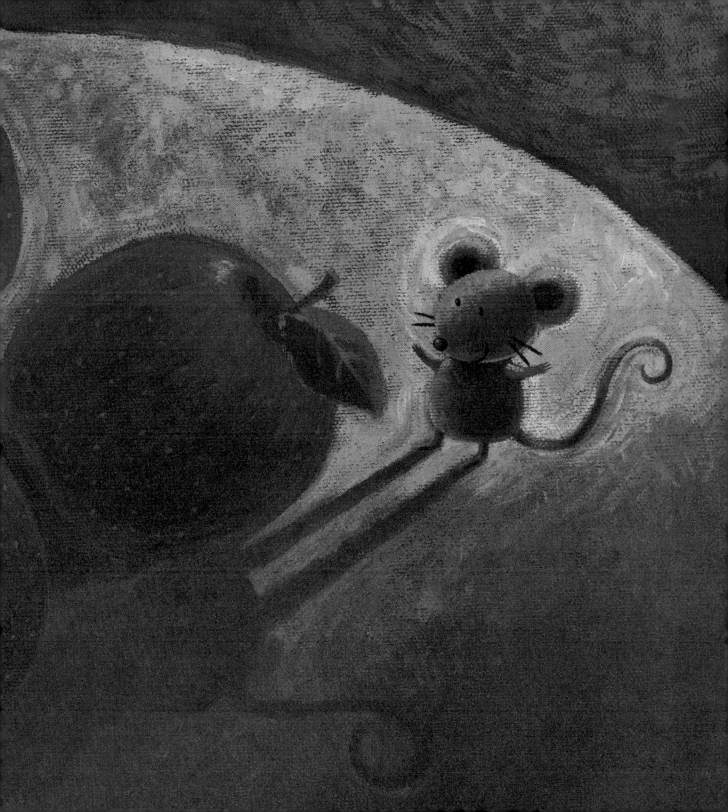

Over near the wall,
Mouse saw
something sneaking—
Creep! Creep! Creep!

"Eeek!"
Mouse
squeaked.

What could it be?

Scampering kittens!
That's all.
Not so scary
after all.

Deep in the shadows,
Mouse saw something flickering—
Grin! Grin! Grin!

"Eeek!"
Mouse
squeaked.

What could it be?

A glowing
jack
- o' -
lantern!

That's all.
Not so scary
after all.

Then, on the step,
Mouse heard something knocking—
Thump! Thump! Thump!

"*Eeek!*"
Mouse
squeaked.

THUMP! THUMP! THUMP!

What, oh, what could it be?

TRICK-OR-TREATERS!

Hooray!

And they sang,
"Trick or treat!
Giggle and fright!
It's fun to be scared...

on Halloween night!"